Run!

By Sue Ferraby

Illustrated by Fabiano Fiorin

Special thanks to our advisers for their expertise:

Adria F. Klein, Ph.D.
Professor Emeritus, California State University
San Bernardino, California

Susan Kesselring, M.A.
Literacy Educator
Rosemount-Apple Valley-Eagan (Minnesota) School District

PiCTURE WiNDOW BOOKS
Minneapolis, Minnesota

Levels for *Read-it!* Readers

- Familiar topics
- Frequently used words
- Repeating patterns

- New ideas
- Larger vocabulary
- Variety of language structures

- Challenges in ideas
- Expanded vocabulary
- Wide variety of sentences

- More complex ideas
- Extended vocabulary range
- Expanded language structures

A Note to Parents and Caregivers:

Read-it! Readers are for children who are just starting on the amazing road to reading. These beautiful books support both the acquisition of reading skills and the love of books.

The RED LEVEL presents familiar topics using common words and repeating sentence patterns.

The BLUE LEVEL presents new ideas using a larger vocabulary and varied sentence structure.

The YELLOW LEVEL presents more challenging ideas, a broad vocabulary, and wide variety in sentence structure.

The GREEN LEVEL presents more complex ideas, an extended vocabulary range, and expanded language structures.

When sharing a book with your child, read in short stretches, pausing often to talk about the pictures. Have your child turn the pages and point to the pictures and familiar words. And be sure to reread favorite stories or parts of stories.

There is no right or wrong way to share books with children. Find time to read with your child, and pass on the legacy of literacy.

Adria F. Klein, Ph.D.
Professor Emeritus
California State University
San Bernardino, California

First American edition published in 2003 by
Picture Window Books
5115 Excelsior Boulevard
Suite 232
Minneapolis, MN 55416
877-845-8392
www.picturewindowbooks.com

First published in Great Britain by Franklin Watts, 96 Leonard Street,
London, EC2A 4XD

Text © Sue Ferraby 2002
Illustration © Fabiano Fiorin 2002

Printed in the United States of America.

Library of Congress Cataloging-in-Publication Data
Ferraby, Sue.
Run! / by Sue Ferraby ; illustrated by Fabio Fiorin.
p. cm. — (Read-it! readers)
Summary: Jonathon the mouse sneaks into a stone house one dark night, but when he tries
to return to his home in the woods he encounters many frightening obstacles.
ISBN 1-4048-0552-4 (hardcover)
[1. Mice—Fiction. 2. Imagination—Fiction. 3. Night—Fiction.] I. Fiorin, Fabiano, ill.
II. Title. III. Series.
PZ7.F3635Ru 2004
[E]—dc22   2004007620

Once a mouse called Jonathon
left his home in the rustling
leaves of the Tangly Wood.

He crawled under the wire fence
and through a grass tunnel
to a little house.

Jonathon climbed the
cold stone steps.

He squeezed under the door.

He tiptoed over the prickly mat
into the kitchen.

All night long he ate crumbs in
the shadows under the stairs.

By and by, the stars faded away. The moon crossed the sky. "I must get home before the sun comes up," thought Jonathon.

Jonathon ran out of the shadows
under the stairs.

But a cat sat on the prickly mat,
so Jonathon couldn't get home.

Jonathon stopped. He listened.
He looked.

Jonathon saw that the cat was really

a coat, dropped in a heap.

Jonathon ran out of the shadows
under the stairs, and across the
prickly mat.

But a giant stood on the cold stone steps, guarding the door. Jonathon couldn't get home.

Jonathon stopped. He listened.
He looked.

He saw that the giant feet were
not feet at all, but a pair of big
boots left outside.

Jonathon ran out of the shadows
under the stairs, across the prickly
mat, and down the cold stone steps.

But a ghost spread its hands over
the grass tunnel, so Jonathon
couldn't get home.

Jonathon stopped. He listened.

He looked.

He saw that the ghost was a piece of
paper, flapping in the wind.

Jonathon ran out of the shadows under the stairs, across the prickly mat, down the cold stone steps, and through the grass tunnel.

But an owl sat near the wire
fence, watching even the smallest
thing that moved.

Jonathon stopped. He listened.
He looked.

The owl looked straight back at him.

Jonathon's heart froze with fear.

Then Jonathon saw that the owl was
the great sun rising through the
branches of the Tangly Wood.
It was morning.

27

Jonathon ran out of the shadows under the stairs, across the prickly mat, down the cold stone steps, through the grass tunnel, and under the wire fence.

Home he ran, to the rustling

leaves of the Tangly Wood,

where he was safe at last.

Levels for *Read-it!* Readers

**Read-it! Readers help children practice early reading
skills with brightly illustrated stories.**

Red Level: Familiar topics with frequently used words and
repeating patterns.

I Am in Charge of Me by Dana Meachen Rau
Let's Share by Dana Meachen Rau

Blue Level: New ideas with a larger vocabulary and a variety
of language structures.

At the Beach by Patricia M. Stockland
The Playground Snake by Brian Moses

Yellow Level: Challenging ideas with an expanded vocabulary
and a wide variety of sentences.

Flynn Flies High by Hilary Robinson
Marvin, the Blue Pig by Karen Wallace
Moo! by Penny Dolan
Pippin's Big Jump by Hilary Robinson
The Queen's Dragon by Anne Cassidy
Sounds Like Fun by Dana Meachen Rau
Tired of Waiting by Dana Meachen Rau
Whose Birthday Is It? by Sherryl Clark

Green Level: More complex ideas with an extended vocabulary
range and expanded language structures.

Clever Cat by Karen Wallace
Flora McQuack by Penny Dolan
Izzie's Idea by Jillian Powell
Naughty Nancy by Anne Cassidy
The Princess and the Frog by Margaret Nash
The Roly-Poly Rice Ball by Penny Dolan
Run! by Sue Ferraby
Sausages! by Anne Adeney
Stickers, Shells, and Snow Globes by Dana Meachen Rau
The Truth About Hansel and Gretel by Karina Law
Willie the Whale by Joy Oades

**A complete list of *Read-it!* Readers is available on our Web site:
www.picturewindowbooks.com**